Mrs McTats
and her Houseful of
Cats

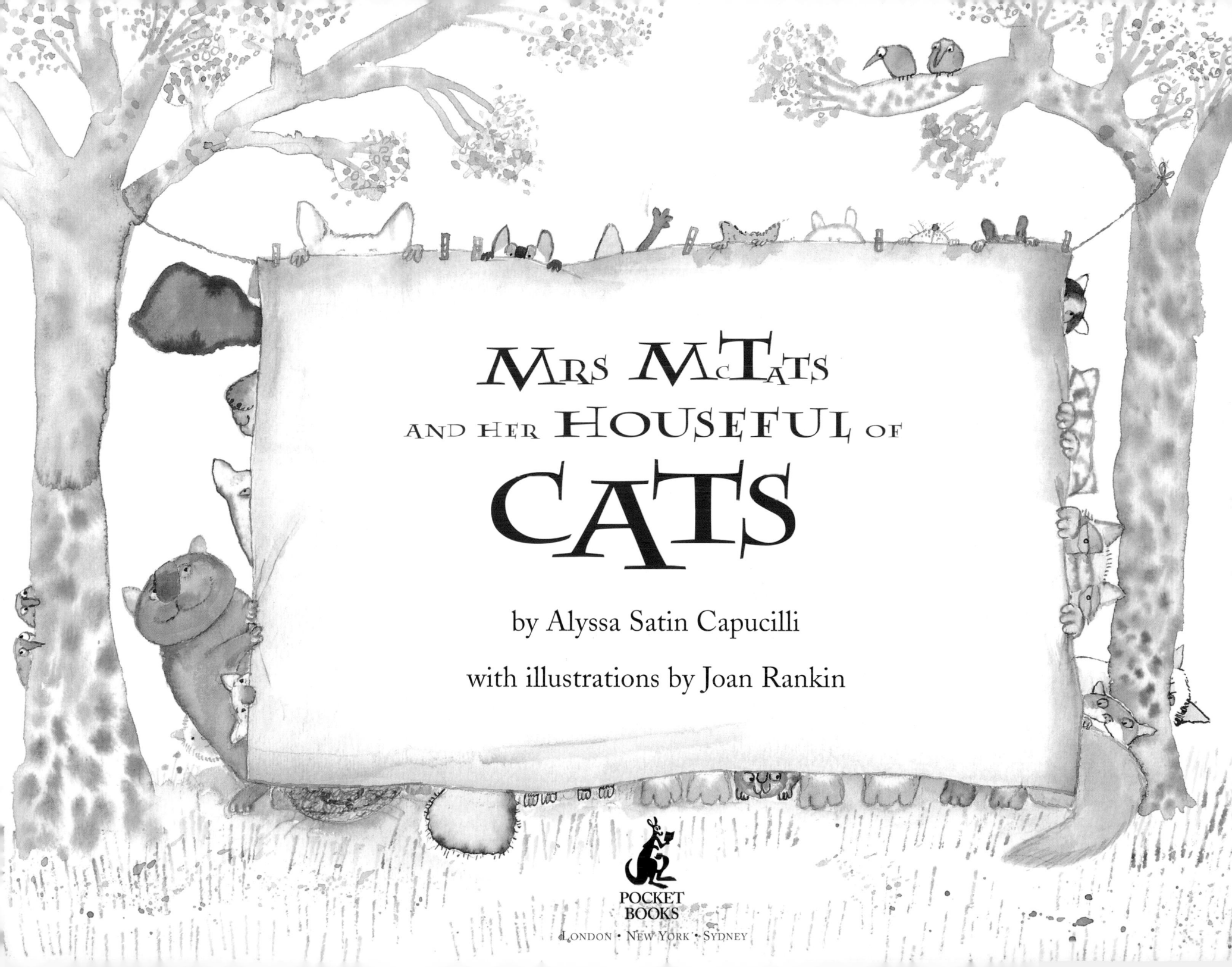

Mrs McTats
and her Houseful of
Cats

by Alyssa Satin Capucilli

with illustrations by Joan Rankin

POCKET
BOOKS
LONDON · NEW YORK · SYDNEY

First published in Great Britain in 2001 by Simon & Schuster UK Ltd
Africa House, 64–78 Kingsway, London WC2B 6AH

This edition published in 2003 by Pocket Books, an imprint of Simon & Schuster UK Ltd.

Originally published in the USA in 2001 by Margaret K. McElderry Books,
an imprint of Simon & Schuster Children's Publishing Division, New York.

A CIP catalogue record for this book is available from the British Library upon request

Book design by Ann Bobco
The text for this book was set in Adobe Caslon.
The illustrations are rendered in watercolour

ISBN 0743462068

Printed in Italy.

3 5 7 9 10 8 6 4 2

For a sweet dear named Liza
– A. S. C.

To Tony, who never turned any cats
away
– J. R.

In a small, cosy cottage
lived Mrs McTats.
She lived all alone,
except for one cat.

Every morning she left
as the clock struck eight –
"To market, to market!
I mustn't be late."

She browsed through the market
and chose a plump fish.
"For **A**bner and me.
What a sumptuous dish!"

But when she got home,
there came a scratch on the door,
and in walked two cats.
Was there room for two more?

"Come in, my sweet dears,"
said Mrs McTats.
"I'm sure I've got room
for just two more cats.

I'll call you Basil,

and Curly you'll be.

I only had one cat,
but now I have three!"

The very next morning
Mrs McTats woke early.
She stopped to pet **A**bner
and **B**asil and **C**urly.

"To market, to market!
I mustn't be late.

This chicken, I think,
will surely taste great."

But when she got home,
there came a scratch on the door,
and in walked three cats.
Was there room for three more?

"Come in, my sweet dears,"
said Mrs McTats.
"I think I've got room
for just three more cats.

Now, give me a moment.
What shall your names be?

You're Dolly,

you're Ernest,

and Fuzzy makes three!"

The very next morning
off went Mrs McTats.
"What can I buy
for my six hungry cats?"

"I've got it!" she said.
"I'll make a nice stew."
So she carried home beef
and liver to brew.

But back at home
there came a scratch on the door,
and in walked four cats.
Was there room for four more?

"Come in, my sweet dears,"
said Mrs McTats.
"I know there's a place
for just four more cats.
Ten's a fine number –
ten cats and me –

I'll call you Goldie

and
Herman
you'll be."

Izzy

and Jezebel

pranced 'cross the floor.
And then, right behind them . . .

. . . followed five more!

"Koko

and Linus,

Millie,

Noreen.

And you shall be Oscar.

There, that makes fifteen!"

The very next day,
off went Mrs McTats.
"What can I possibly
feed fifteen cats?"

She chose a fresh tuna.

She chose a fine trout.

But when she got home,
her cats were all out!

She counted her cats
from one to fifteen,
but somehow six more cats
had just joined the scene!
"Come, come, my sweet dears,"
said Mrs McTats.
"I'm sure I have plenty
for twenty-one cats.

Pip,

Quip,

and **R**osebud.

Sally

and Toesie.

Ursula, dear,
do make yourself cosy."

But then came another
scratch on the door.

Could it be more cats?
How many more?

In came **V**iolet.

In came **W**innie.

And, just behind,
a kitten she named **X**innie.

In came **Y**odel –
the last of the bunch.

Twenty-five cats
ready for lunch!

But something was missing.
What could it be?
Just what it was,
Mrs McTats could not see.
As she stood there puzzling,
there was a scratch on the door
and Mrs McTats wondered,
Could there really be more?
Could she squeeze in more cats?
More than twenty-five?
Who was the one
who was next to arrive?

"Come in, my sweet dear,"
said Mrs McTats.
"I live in this cottage with
twenty-five cats.
But if you don't mind,
you're welcome to stay.
You're welcome to eat.
You're welcome to play."

Now in that small cottage
lives Mrs McTats,
all happy and cosy with her
twenty-five cats . . .

. . . and one little puppy,
who's known as Zoom,
in a small, cosy cottage
with plenty of room.

And just when the clock
strikes each morning at eight,
Mrs McTats hurries off.
"I mustn't be late!

To market, to market!
What treats will there be?
For twenty-six sweet dears
from A to Z !"